FIZZOPOLIS

The Trouble with
FUZZWONKER FIZZ

for Noah and Ella!

PATRICK CARMAN

Illustrated by
BRIAN SHEESLEY

KATHERINE TEGEN BOOKS
An Imprint of HarperCollins Publishers

Katherine Tegen Books is an imprint of
HarperCollins Publishers.

Fizzopolis: The Trouble with Fuzzwonker Fizz
Text copyright © 2016 by Patrick Carman
Illustrations copyright © 2016 by Brian Sheesley

Library of Congress Cataloging-in-Publication Data
Carman, Patrick.
  The trouble with Fuzzwonker Fizz / by Patrick Carman ;
illustrated by Brian Sheesley. — First edition.
    pages cm. — (Fizzopolis ; [1])
  Summary: Ten-year-old Harold, the adopted son of a food
inventor, discovers that his father's latest invention, soda pop
that produces the world's longest burps, also generates furry
creatures known as Fizzies.
  ISBN 978-0-06-239390-6 (hardcover)
  [1. Inventions—Fiction. 2. Imaginary creatures—Fiction.
3. Humorous stories.] I. Sheesley, Brian, illustrator. II. Title.
PZ7.C21694Tt 2016   2015010021
[Fic]—dc23   CIP
                                                              AC

Typography by Joel Tippie
16 17 18 19 20   CG/RRDH   10 9 8 7 6 5 4 3 2 1
❖
First Edition

For ~~Harold~~ Floyd, the most amazing
stunt kid in the world
—P.C.

For Joni,
My Love.
My Life.
My Laughter . . .
—B.S.

CHAPTER 1

Hi, I'm Harold Fuzzwonker. I'm the one with the zippy striped shirt, the huge grin from ear to ear, and the really long arm. I'm riding one of my favorite things in the world: my red bike.

"I'm coming in hot!" I screamed, pedaling like a wild banshee. In one hand, I held a milk shake.

I could hear the assembled crowd of two people talking about me as I raced by.

"That Fuzzwonker kid is a real airhead," Jeff Flasky, an annoying neighbor of mine, said.

A girl I'd never met before came to my

defense. I'd seen her at my last event, though. She was new in town.

"Not true!" she said. "Harold Fuzzwonker is the most dangerous daredevil in Pflugerville. I saw him jump over a swimming pool last week."

"It was a kiddie pool," Jeff Flasky said. "And it was filled with pillows."

"He's gonna make it!" the girl shouted as I approached the ramp.

She was sitting on a green bike with a banana seat and a sissy bar. If it was my bike, I'd call it the Dill Pickle.

"If you say so," Jeff Flasky said. He shrugged his shoulders and his giant head wobbled back and forth. Flasky's got a real noggin on him.

It's at least two sizes too big for the rest of Jeff Flasky.

I took a sip of the milk shake and pedaled even faster.

did I get this right?

"He really is coming in hot," the girl said.

"Like a blowtorch," Flasky agreed.

"And one-handed. The real deal."

Those were the last words I heard as my front wheel hit the wobbly ramp, and I was airborne. The world went into slow-mo as I glided above my dad's car. Everything was going exactly like I had planned until I sailed

over the handlebars and landed on the pavement in a pool of milk shake.

"Whoa!" the girl yelled.

"What an airhead," Jeff Flasky said.

I stuck my tongue out and licked some of the milk shake off the driveway.

The next thing I remember, I was lying in bed with an ice pack as big as a watermelon balanced on top of my head. I popped the top on a bottle of Fuzzwonker Fizz and guzzled the contents down in one gulp. Then I burped for nine seconds in a row.

"What a dud," I said, looking at the bottle.

My dad, Dr. Fuzzwonker, invented this amazing soda pop that will give you the biggest, longest burps in the world (it's super-popular stuff, as you can probably imagine).

He adopted me when I was a teensy-weensy bundle of baby. We live together in the town of Pflugerville in an ordinary-looking house. My dad spends a lot of his time in the top secret basement. I haven't been down there. It's *that* secret.

"You tried to jump over the car again, didn't you?" Dr. Fuzzwonker asked.

"I did."

We both looked out my bedroom window, where Jeff Flasky and the girl I didn't know were standing on the sidewalk. Flasky was holding a sign that said *Harold = Stoopid*. The girl had a sign, too. That one said *Do It Again!*

"Your fans?" my dad asked.

I shrugged and the watermelon-sized bag of ice almost fell off my head. "I'm a polarizing figure, Dad. What can I say? It's part of my persona."

My dad's gaze landed on the pavement. "Is that my milk shake?"

I smiled like a goofball.

"I'll get you another one!"

I could see the wheels turning in my dad's head. He was imagining me jumping over a row of garbage cans and crashing through the front window of our house.

"Isn't nine a little young for a daredevil?" he asked me.

"Dad, I'm ten," I said. "How else would I have these huge muscles?"

I sat up in bed and flexed, producing a tiny bump in the middle of my noodle arm. It was about the size of a marble.

Dr. Fuzzwonker moved swiftly to my bed for a closer look at my mega monster muscle.

"Good gravy gobblers,

you *are* ten! You've got some real live muscle there. Do you realize what this means? It means something BIG. I've been saving a present for your tenth birthday. And here you are, *already* ten!"

I've gotten used to the idea that Dr. Fuzzwonker is brilliant but scatterbrained. He sometimes forgets things (like how old I am).

"I get to drive the car!" I yelled.

"Not a chance," Dr. Fuzzwonker said. He folded his arms across his chest and acted like I would never guess what it was.

I took the bag of ice off my head and pulled my hat down close to my ears, thinking. I never take my hat off unless I go scuba diving or waterskiing (two things I have never done), or when my dad makes me take a shower. I'm not a fan of showers. I wish Dr. Fuzzwonker would use a water bazooka and hose me down in the backyard in my polka-dot Bermuda shorts.

"You got me a dinosaur!" I yelled.

"We've talked about this a thousand times," Dr. Fuzzwonker answered.

"You can't have a dinosaur until you're twelve. It's a big responsibility."

I scratched my hat. I was running out of ideas. "A flying motorcycle?"

"Not even close!" Dr. Fuzzwonker said, his eyes growing wide with excitement.

"How about a titanium robot that fights evil space lobsters?" I asked. "Is that it?"

"You know I haven't finished the Lobstrobot yet."

"Argh. Is it a Homework Completor 4000?

I've been asking for one of those for at least ten thousand years."

"Still working on it."

"What is it? Tell me!"

Dr. Fuzzwonker leaned in close and paused and smiled and raised his eyebrows.

"I'm giving you something better than all those things put together. I'm giving you . . . a JOB!"

I had a vision of standing on an assembly line, making loopy women's earrings or sorting through a conveyer belt of rotten fruit or cutting the grass on a football field with a pair of fingernail clippers.

"I'm only ten!" I shouted. "You *can't* give me a job!"

But Dr. Fuzzwonker wasn't done telling me everything about my long-awaited present.

"Come along, my freshly minted ten-year-old. Your job is in the *basement*."

That was when I jumped out of bed like a monkey struck by lightning.

Here's a little bit about Dr. Fuzz-wonker before I go on with the basement situation.

While Dr. Fuzzwonker may look like a normal doctor, he is not. He's a food doctor. I know what you're thinking. Dr. Fuzzwonker fixes broken French fries and performs surgery on donuts.

No! What Dr. Fuzzwonker does is even better than that. He invents weird stuff to eat and drink. Like Fuzz-wonker Fizz, the most popular kids' pop in the world. Fuzzwonker Fizz packs twenty essential vitamins and minerals into a sweet-tasting, totally sugar-free celebration for your taste buds.

But that's not why everyone in Pflugerville loves it so much.

Fuzzwonker Fizz is so popular because it makes the longest burps in the history of ever. They last, on average, fourteen seconds.

The longest, loudest Fuzzwonker Fizz burp ever officially recorded was produced by Lucy Detmyer when she was ten. Lucy's burp lasted twenty-seven seconds and sounded like a lawn mower.

It was bubble-gum flavored. Lucy got a Fuzzwonker Fizz endorsement deal for that burp. And her own flavor: Lucy Lemon.

Another famous recorded burp came from Carlyle Spunkman. He was driving in the car with his mom when he downed a whole bottle of Fuzzwonker Fizz and "AAARP!" The loudest burp in all of recorded-history-since-before-the-Romans came out of his mouth. Although it's only a rumor, some people say the car windows exploded. Another unconfirmed rumor about Carlyle's burp: The family cat was in the car and has since gone completely deaf from the magnitude of that amazing moment of burpdom.

Dr. Fuzzwonker gave Spunkman his own flavor, too: Spunky Strawberry.

RRRRRRRR R RR RRI

So I was jumping up and down on my bed, and my head was almost hitting the ceiling. I was *that* excited to finally see the super-secret-Fuzzwonker basement.

"I need to finish some taste testing," Dr. Fuzzwonker said. He looked at his watch. "Meet me in the kitchen in thirty-seven point three seconds."

I did a bunch of somersaults and cartwheels down the hallway and arrived in the kitchen four minutes late.

Dr. Fuzzwonker waited for me next to the refrigerator. He was swirling up some kind of crazy vegetable drink in our Blend-O-Matic. There were two glasses, and he poured half of whatever this stuff was into each one. It was lumpy, orange, and foamy.

"I'm going with waffles," I said, grabbing a cold one from a stack on a plate. "You can have my half. I don't mind."

RRRRRRRRRRRRRRR

"Why, thank you," my dad said, and then he chugged both glasses in two seconds flat.

He opened the refrigerator door and reached way back, past a cantaloupe, around a teetering stack of chocolate donuts, back, back, and still back farther, where a very old bottle of hot sauce was hiding in the farthest corner.

He turned toward me, suddenly as serious as an Oxford dictionary.

"Everything you see, from this point on, is a Fuzzwonker family trust. It's *secret*. This is not a little secret, it's a BIG one. The biggest one there is! Even people in the Pentagon don't know about this stuff. Even the Navy SEALs and the president can't know about it. Even if aliens arrive and blow everyone away with lasers and only you and one other person remain on the planet, you

RRRRRRRRRRRRRRRRRRRRRRRRRRRRRRRRRRRR

still can't speak a word about what's hidden in the basement. EVEN IF—"

"I get it," I interrupted. "Don't tell my buddies at school."

"Exactly!"

I nodded and picked up another leftover waffle from the counter. I'd better fill up the tank in case my dad makes me work for five hundred hours without a break. It could happen.

Dr. Fuzzwonker twisted the bottle of hot sauce. Three times one way, then back again twice.

"Hot SAWCE," he said, then jumped back, slammed the door of the refrigerator shut, and picked up his coffee mug.

I put an entire waffle in my mouth and reached for the door.

HERE
LIES
LUCY'S
BURP

RRRRRrrrrrrrrrrrrppppppppp
This is where Lucy's
27 second burp died.

"Better not touch that," Dr. Fuzzwonker said, sipping his coffee. "It's dangerous."

I needed some milk, badly, but we didn't have any in the fridge. The waffle was drier than a mouthful of powdered soap and it was clogging up my windpipe, so I turned on the water at the sink and leaned over the counter. My mouth felt like it was full of wet cement, but I didn't mind. I was going to the basement!

When I turned back, the refrigerator had moved four feet to the left. I reached down and picked up a purple sock covered in dust bunnies.

"I'm guessing this belongs to you?" I asked.

Dr. Fuzzwonker took off his left shoe.

"Socks are so hard to keep track of, don't you agree?" Dr. Fuzzwonker said.

Dr. Fuzzwonker put his lost sock back on and then put his shoe back on, and then the wall opened up like an elevator door.

"Go ahead, get in. We've got work to do!" Dr. Fuzzwonker said.

And so it was that I, Harold Fuzzwonker, was introduced to my dad's secret elevator, which led to an even secreter secret.

"You're going to want to start chewing this," my dad said, handing me a foot-long stick of gum. It was the biggest piece of gum I'd ever seen.

"Oh yeah! Is this a new product test? Hmm. Let's see. Well . . ."

"Keep chewing."

"Dad, this is just regular bubble gum," I said, but the wad of gum was about the size of a baseball, so it came out like, "Phap oof egg bubb mmmmm?"

"We're not conducting a taste test today, newly minted employee," my dad said. "Also you're slobbering on my shoe."

I was very interested in whatever gross, weird, irresponsible shenanigans were going on in the basement of the Fuzzwonker house. My job was going to give me a peek into the super-secret laboratory where Fuzzwonker Fizz was created! Maybe I wouldn't have to do any work at all. Maybe I'd get a lab coat and test new candy and bigger burps. Yeah! That had to be it!

"Keep chewing," he reminded me again.

And so I did.

Dr. Fuzzwonker got into the elevator with me and stared at the buttons. I read the words above each level of the basement.

Way down there.

Wow, this is really far under the house.

Holy dirt mouse, Fuzzwonker! Much farther and you'll hit China!

"Please spit your gum into your hand," Dr. Fuzzwonker said. "You're going to need it to bypass our first security protocol."

I started to ask what to hold on to, because the elevator was nothing but four walls, three buttons, and a ceiling. Dr. Fuzzwonker grabbed a huge glob of previously chewed gum off the side of the elevator and stuck it to his shoe.

What the heck?

He nodded for me to do the same. The second I got my giant wad of gum on my shoe and stuck it on the floor, he hit button number three, and it was like someone had cut the rope that held up the elevator. I screamed. My arms flew up into the air, but my foot stayed glued to the floor.

"What if my shoe comes off?" I yelled.

"Curl your toes, newbie. You'll be fine," my dad said calmly.

Down the elevator went, faster and faster, until it passed *Wow, this is really far under the house* with a pleasant *ding!*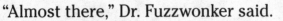

"Almost there," Dr. Fuzzwonker said.

When the elevator came to a stop and I was sure we weren't going any farther, my stomach crawled down from my throat.

Dr. Fuzzwonker and I took the gum off our shoes and stored both wads on the wall.

"This is super gross," I said.

"I know. Isn't it the best?" Dr. Fuzzwonker smiled.

I had to agree. It was totally awesome.

"Remember now," Dr. Fuzzwonker said. "Everything behind this door is *seeeeeecret.*"

I gulped like there was a boiled egg caught in my windpipe.

I was finally going to see the basement.

CHAPTER 3

I waited for the doors of the elevator to open and thought about what might be hiding on the other side. Dr. Fuzzwonker had always been unpredictable when it came to inventing things, and this made me nervous.

Once, when I was four, Dr. Fuzzwonker made a ball of saltwater taffy almost as big as the house. He made it in the backyard, where it spread out and ate my tricycle, my jungle gym, and three cats.

It took an hour and a half to get the cats out, and we had to shave all three of them bald to keep them from sticking to the furniture.

That ball of taffy darn near ate *me* when I got too close and tried to touch it. We were lucky it didn't roll down the street and eat some cars and garbage cans.

"Are you ready for your first day of work?" Dr. Fuzzwonker asked.

"I have no idea," I said as I thought about the house-sized ball of taffy and shivered.

"Prepare to be wowed," Dr. Fuzzwonker said. "You are about to see . . . FIZZOPOLIS!"

The doors opened and I looked out over Fizzopolis for the first time. It was a vast underground habitat filled with color and light.

Conveyer belts zigzagged in every direction, carrying Fuzzwonker Fizz bottles. In the middle of the space was a gigantic machine with pipes and tubes and buttons and levers.

"That's the Fizzomatic machine," Dr. Fuzzwonker said.

"You've been busy down here," I marveled.

Dr. Fuzzwonker grabbed a bottle of Fuzzwonker Fizz rolling by, popped the top, and guzzled it down. He burped for twelve seconds.

"Good one," I said.

Dr. Fuzzwonker looked at the bottle. "One of my greatest inventions, don't you think?"

A furry creature about the same size as me waddled by. It made a fizzy sound as it went, and little bits of neon green confetti trailed behind it.

I was starting to get used to the idea that Fizzopolis was going to be full of surprises, but I still threw my hands in the air and ran around in circles like an idiot.

"This is nuts!" I said, because you know, an ALIEN CREATURE had just walked by.

I took a closer look around and realized there were furry creatures *everywhere*.

What the—

"The Fizzomatic doesn't just make Fuzz-wonker Fizz," my dad said. "It also makes Fizzies."

"Fizzies?" I asked. "What's a Fizzy?"

"Why sure, Fizzies. Walk with me."

Dr. Fuzzwonker talked while we walked.

"I began my work as a food-mad scientist when I was ten, just like you. I loved to mix potions and make poofs of smoke and produce small zaps of lightning."

We passed under a big tree with looping limbs.

"Did you learn that stuff from your dad?" I asked.

"Actually, it all started with my dad's dad, Fuzzwonker Senior. He owned a restaurant that specialized in noodles. It was called Seldoon. That's "noodles" spelled backward. Seldoon had every kind of noodle imaginable, and I was a noodle experimenter from the start. I made all sorts of gizmos and gadgets that helped Fuzzwonker Senior create the best noodle dishes in town. We made the longest noodle in

the history of the world—seven miles—which
I ate in one sitting."

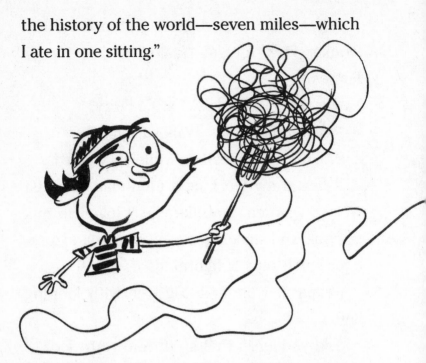

"Impressive!" I said. We walked by a cave
that led into blackness. I shivered, but Dr.
Fuzzwonker kept going.

"When I got older, I went to mixing school,
science school, eating school, and candy
school. Then I dug a giant hole under our
house and went straight to work on Fuzzwonker Fizz. I built a machine with a lot of
dials and levers and buttons and tubes and
called it the Fizzomatic.

"There are holes in the machine for dropping things inside like pogo sticks, golf balls, and bananas."

"You do realize this all sounds crazy," I said.

Dr. Fuzzwonker ignored me. He was on a roll.

"At first, things didn't go so well. I added a lemon, a Frisbee, a Ping-Pong ball, and a fire hydrant to the Fizzomatic. I got a soda pop that tasted like an egg roll–flavored pancake."

"Gross."

"But the next day I added a lightbulb, a

candy cane, a skateboard, and a watermelon and PA-RESTO: Out came a new flavor of soda! Unfortunately, that one tasted like a sandwich made of shag carpet."

"Dad, this story is getting really weird."

Dr. Fuzzwonker yelled. "Kids didn't want soda that tasted like shag carpet. What was I missing? I redoubled my efforts. Snarfballs!"

"Then what happened?" I asked.

"Then came the day when I produced a nine-second cherry-flavored burp, which I burped right into a tube that sent all sorts of burp data into a burp-analyzing computer. When I saw the information it produced, I knew I was ninety-nine percent finished with the first batch of Fuzzwonker Fizz."

"What about that last one percent?" I asked.

"Ninety-nine ingredients were just right, but I couldn't figure out the final item that would create the perfect soda pop. I tried a ballpoint pen, a basketball, and an electric guitar. None of them worked. That was when something miraculous happened."

We came alongside some strange plant with all sorts of vines, and Dr. Fuzzwonker knelt down with a pair of toenail clippers and clipped a small leaf. He put it in his pocket.

"Don't leave me hangin'!" I said. "What happened?"

"I used a dash of chili powder, which I didn't hold out much hope for, and BAM! Instead of a beaker full of fizzy liquid, what came out of the Fizzomatic machine was . . . well, it was . . . it was alive!"

"Huh?" I said.

"*It* was Phil," Dr. Fuzzwonker said. "Phil was a shape-shifting blob of goop covered in a thin layer of soft fur. It was the first fizzy creature to pop out of the Fizzomatic machine. He was orange."

"Whoa, Dad. This is incredible!"

"Phil ate the container he
had fallen into. He got a little bigger then, but not too
much, and I thought it was
a good trick. I would later
discover that
Phil could eat
lots of things,
like dirt
and rocks."

Dr. Fuzzwonker kept adding
ingredients to the Fizzomatic machine, and
each time he did, it produced another furry
critter.

"I call them Fizzies," Dr. Fuzzwonker said.

Even long after he had perfected the final
Fuzzwonker Fizz recipe—those hundred
perfect ingredients that could be flavored a
hundred different ways—he kept on making
Fizzies.

There were tall Fizzies and short Fizzies.
They were yellow or lime green or a lot of

other colors. Three Fizzies had polka dots; two of them had stripes.

You just never knew what kind of Fizzy the Fizzomatic was going to spit out next.

After a while, Dr. Fuzzwonker found himself with a hundred Fizzies hidden under the house. So he had Phil dig deeper and deeper and wider and wider, until one day . . .

"I've created a self-sustaining, subterranean, creature-containing world of my

own . . . and it shall be called: FIZZOPOLIS!"
Dr. Fuzzwonker shouted.

And that's how Fizzopolis came into existence. Phil kept on digging and eating, making the habitat bigger and bigger. And some of the other strange creatures, especially the ones with lots of arms, helped Dr. Fuzzwonker build Fizzopolis.

By the time Dr. Fuzzwonker told me all this, we were standing in front of a swampy lagoon, where a slurping creature stood on the shore slurping up green water with a goop-sucking hose. The hose was also the creature's nose.

"Hi, Franny," Dr. Fuzzwonker said. "This is Harold. He's the new assistant. Also my son."

Franny smiled as she got bigger and bigger, like a balloon filling up, and then all the green water reversed direction like it was coming out of a fire hose.

It made a gloppity-gloop-gloop sound that's

probably one of the top
three sounds I have ever
heard. Franny lost con-
trol of her nose hose. The

water jet, which had been turned from green
to clean, pointed at me. It hit me like a cannon-
ball, and I tumbled backward until I came to
rest against one of the outer
walls of Fizzopolis.

"Remember,
Franny," Dr. Fuzzwonker
said. "You need to hold the nose
hose first, *then* release. Let's work on that."

Franny made snurfing and snoodling noises
and walked over to me. She took in a gigantic breath of air and aimed her nose hose at
my head. When Franny let loose, it was like
the dryer in a car wash, and I was plastered
against the wall like a bug in a windstorm.

I rolled around like a marble in a tornado, and when she finished, my hair was standing straight up on my head.

"This is the best day in the history of my life!" I yelled.

"Sorry for soaking you," Franny said. She had a watery sort of voice, like she was plugging her nose hose. She mumbled instructions to herself. "First I hold on to the nose hose, *then* I blast the swamp. It's a lot to remember."

"How about if I help you with that?" I offered. "Let's try it again."

And so we did, but this time, I held her nose like a fire hose and everything went swimmingly.

"The lagoon needs cleaning twice a week," Dr. Fuzzwonker said. "That means all the water must be turned from green to clean.

Think you two can handle it?"

Franny blew her nose in the air, which made a honking sound like a goose, and then she nodded and smiled.

"We got this, Dad," I said. "No problem."

Dr. Fuzzwonker pulled a notepad and a pencil out of his white mad-scientist lab coat and made a check mark.

"Moving on, then," he said as he walked deeper into Fizzopolis and stood in front of a giant yellow clump of fur. "This is George."

I put my hand out and petted George. He wobbled sideways and made a sound like the fizz after a soda pop is poured over ice. It was tingly on my hand.

"He likes you," my dad said.

"Ya think?"

"Oh yes. When Fizzies don't like someone, they zap."

"You mean like static electricity?"

"I mean like an electric fence."

"Double whoa!" I said. I started to realize that Fizzopolis was more dangerous than I thought. And more awesome.

"Playtime is over, George. Time to go back to your cave."

The yellow clump of fur, about the size of a car, started rolling away. It flopped and wobbled as it went.

"George doesn't talk much, but he's friendly. You'll like him."

I looked down at the green grassy spot where George had been playing.

"Hey, George!" I yelled. I leaned over and picked up a yellow rubber ducky. "You forgot your toy!"

George stopped flopping and rolling. He appeared to be waiting.

"You can throw it," Dr. Fuzzwonker said.

I reeled back and threw the rubber ducky as hard as I could. It was a high, wild throw that sailed ten feet over George. But George stretched his yellow furry blobby body up into the air and caught the ducky. Then he rolled away.

Dr. Fuzzwonker made another check on his list.

"He forgets his toy about three times a week."

"Got it!" I said.

We wandered past a Ping-Pong table, where a lanky Fizzy with four long arms played both sides of the table.

"Leroy doesn't like to share the Ping-Pong table," Dr. Fuzzwonker said. "He needs a strict four-hour limit per day."

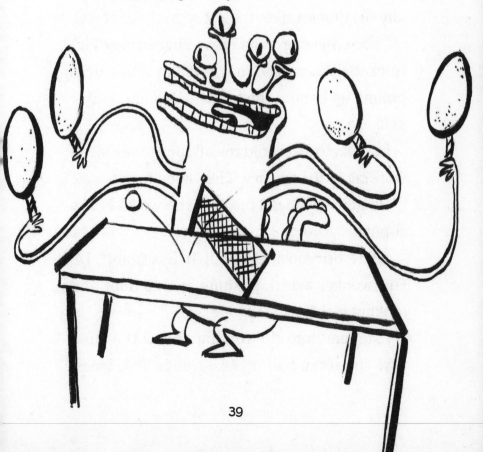

"Work on sharing, no problemo," I said.

On and on we went, through all the different parts of Fizzopolis, discovering the many things that needed doing. There were Fizzies everywhere, and peculiar habitats made of sagging, twisting tree limbs. There were giant loopy-limbed trees and caves and vines. Conveyer belts ran all over the place, high up into the ceiling of Fizzopolis, where they eventually disappeared on their way to the surface.

"The conveyer belts move Fuzzwonker Fizz from the Fizzomatic machine out into trucks pulling up behind the house," Dr. Fuzzwonker said.

Dr. Fuzzwonker told me all the Fizzies loved working in the factory. They lived for it!

He guided me deeper into the world of Fizzopolis.

"How do you feel about babysitting?" Dr. Fuzzwonker asked, pushing open a door and looking inside.

I stepped into the room and saw the nursery. The room had rocks, strange little trees, and a kiddie pool. And there were three tiny Fizzies, wrestling around on the floor like kittens. One was pink, one was purple, and one was orange.

They all looked up at me, wide-eyed and nervous.

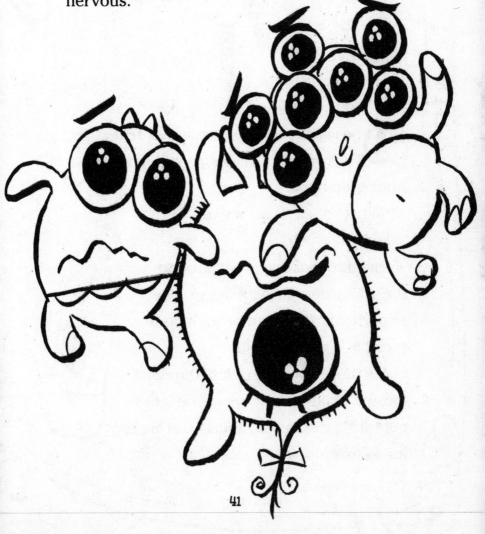

CHAPTER 4

"**D**on't make any sudden movements," Dr. Fuzzwonker said. "They'll go bonkers on you."

"What does that mean?" I asked.

Dr. Fuzzwonker glanced around the room nervously. "There's one in particular that can be . . . unpredictable. The green one."

All three kiddie Fizzies stared at me with big round eyes. They were cute little creatures, and I bent down for a closer look.

"That's Bob, Ethel, and Ruth," Dr. Fuzz-wonker said, pointing to the orange one, the purple one, and the pink one.

"I don't see a green one," I said.

Something darted from one side of the room to the other, but it was so fast all I saw was a flash. Whatever it was, it hid behind a boulder sitting in the corner of the room. Its head peeked out, and I saw a small horn and huge oval eyes.

It was green.

"There he is!" I shouted as I jumped up and down. It was a sudden movement if ever there was one, and all three of the Fizzies

leaped into
the air
and began
bouncing off
the walls. Dr. Fuzz-
wonker didn't move;
he let them bounce off
his head, his elbows,
and his knees. He'd
seen this before. But I
felt like I was in the all-
time best dodgeball
game. I dodged and
ducked and flipped
and twisted.

"That all you got!" I laughed, narrowly avoid-
ing them until all three baby Fizzies tired out
and sat down. They cheered and hollered at
me from the side.

"This babysitting gig is fun!" I said, turning
to my dad just as the small green creature
moved with lightning speed. He was way
faster than the other three, and before I knew

what had happened, the little guy had landed on the side of my head like a glob of peanut butter.

GLORP!

"That would be Floyd," Dr. Fuzz-wonker said. "He's the unpredictable one."

"So I see," I said. Floyd was digging his three-fingered hand into my ear.

"There's nothing in there worth finding," I said. "At least I don't think there is."

Floyd slid under my hat and milled around in my hair, then came out the other side and sat on my shoulder.

He wasn't much bigger than a hamster.

"Does it talk?" I asked.

Floyd grabbed my ear and looked inside, poking his eyeball about halfway inside my head.

And then Floyd spoke, very quietly, so that

only I could hear him. I looked at my dad.

"He says he needs to use the bathroom. And he's thirsty. Also bored."

Dr. Fuzzwonker headed for the door. "That sounds like a list of baby-sitting tasks to me. Have a good time! And try not to break anything."

The-intergalactic-book-of-world-records-across-all-space-and-time lists my first day in Fizzopolis as the BEST DAY AT WORK EVER IN THE HISTORY OF JOBS. We started at the Ping-Pong table, where Floyd and I refereed a Fizzy tournament between four competitive Fizzies: Martha, Leroy, Patrick, and Yam. When all the Ping-Pong balls ended up in the lagoon, we used Floyd as the ball and that added a new dimension to the game. The Fizzies loved it.

"Look how high he goes!" Martha yelled. She had a long neck that expanded and contracted like an accordion, so her head could follow Floyd all the way up into the rafters. Apparently, they had long conversations up there about baseball cards and cotton candy.

"Pancake!" Patrick yelled. He loved it when he slammed his paddle down on Floyd and smashed him on the table. Like a pancake.

"Maybe we shouldn't smoosh the ball like that," I advised Patrick. "It probably doesn't feel very good."

But then Floyd would pop right back up and grin from ear to ear.

Leroy had the advantage of having four arms. They were each about twelve feet long, and he dragged them around like fire hoses when he walked.

"The championship round will be Leroy against . . . Leroy!" I announced when we came to the end. Martha, Patrick, and Yam were all happy to cheer, and then a whole bunch more Fizzies took a break from work to watch. There was a lot of clapping, stomping, and cheering.

It was extremely close, but in the end, Leroy won.

"Come on, Floyd," I said when the tournament ended. "We need to retrieve all the Ping-Pong balls from the lagoon."

We both put on swamp-scuba gear and snorkeled into the water. Franny sucked up a huge glob of air and blew a monster wave, and I rode it like a pro surfer on Zuma Beach. Floyd grabbed a hold of my face and wouldn't let go.

After we found the Ping-Pong balls, Yam took us for a tour around the rest of Fizzopolis. Yam didn't talk. She made squishy Yam sounds and did a lot of pointing, but Floyd sat on my shoulder and translated into my ear. Bright orange fizz popped in the air around Yam as she showed us around.

"That's Dr. Fuzzwonker's laboratory," Floyd said in his squeaky voice. He sounded like a mouse who was also a monkey. I looked up and saw the most outrageous tree house I'd ever seen. It was up in a tall tree that had long green limbs. The laboratory looked like it had been cobbled together, getting bigger and bigger, and each new section was a different color. It also looked like it might fall out of the tree at any time.

Yam took us past caves where the Fizzies lived and waterfalls and groves of little trees with tiny lemons, oranges, and apples.

"She wants you to try one," Floyd said. Yam was staring at one of the small apple trees. It stood only about two feet tall, and the apples were the size of marbles. I took one off the tree and used one tooth to gnaw around the outside.

"Yowza!" I yelled. My lips puckered and I felt like I'd just eaten three cans of frozen apple juice concentrate in a single bite.

"You should try the lemons," Floyd said. "They'll turn your lips inside out."

"Sour?"

Yam nodded and Floyd explained. "This is one of the secrets of Fuzzwonker Fizz. Big flavors in small packages."

"Cool," I said.

Floyd jumped down and took a lemon the size of a jelly bean in his paw. Yam shook her head like it was a bad idea to eat one, but I already knew Floyd well enough to know this would only make him want to eat it more. He tossed it in the air and I reached out to grab it before it could fall into his open mouth, which had grown to the size of a basketball hoop.

Floyd was like that—he could stretch and shrink like you wouldn't believe. I put the jelly bean–size lemon in my pocket, but when I looked back at Floyd, he had taken ten more and tossed those into the air.

"Nice try, little dude!" I said. I captured nine of them out of the air before they could rain down into Floyd's mouth, but I missed the last one. When he ate it, his eyes bulged to about twelve times their normal size, his cheeks punched out like a blowfish, and he made a strange noise like a car rolling down a gravel road. Then he started shaking.

"Hey, little buddy," I said, leaning down real close. "Are you okay?"

Floyd's mouth opened up, and I am not kidding when I say this: He breathed yellow fire. The yellow fire was rocket fuel, and he went flying through the air like a balloon that had been blown up really big and then let go before it was tied.

"What should we do?" I asked Yam. Yam shrugged like she had no idea.

"Incoming!" I shouted, pushing Yam onto the ground as Floyd came in like a bowling ball covered in fire. He barely missed us, then bounced like a Super Ball and pinged off the ceiling. Eventually, the lemon wore off and he rolled in our direction. Smoke poured from his ears.

"Wow, Floyd. Are you okay?" I asked. I thought for sure my buddy would need an emergency room visit. But he smiled and looked longingly at the short lemon trees.

"Oh no you don't," I warned him. "No more goofing off. We've got work to do. This is my job, after all."

Floyd acted all bent out of shape, and he jumped back onto my shoulder. He called me a party pooper, but then he hugged me right around the side of my head.

"You're my best good buddy," I said.

"You're mine, too," Floyd agreed.

We babysat little Fizzies, swept the conveyor belts, organized a Fuzzwonker Fizz bottle cleaning party, and a thousand other things. And all the while Floyd and I were inseparable!

Floyd became extremely upset when I went back upstairs that night. He ate all the Ping-Pong balls, hid George's rubber ducky, and threw dirt clods into the lagoon. Plus a lot of other naughty things a Fizzy shouldn't do.

Dr. Fuzzwonker was super busy creating a brand-new product: furry candy. It was going to be the smash-hit follow-up to Fuzzwonker Fizz. Not only was furry candy going to come in a thousand flavors, it was going to be FURRY! Very exciting, if you ask me.

"Maybe Floyd should sleep in my room tonight," I suggested.

Dr. Fuzzwonker didn't even look up from his furry candy work when he answered.

"Make sure no one sees him. And keep him away from my sock drawer."

It would have been wise to imagine what might happen when Monday morning showed up. That was only one day away, and I would have to go back to Pflugerville Elementary School.

Fizzy-sized trouble was just around the corner.

BUUURRRRRRRRRRRR

CHAPTER 5

I finished my work in Fizzopolis on Sunday, and when Floyd was using the bathroom, I ran to the elevator. I rode to the kitchen and ate pancakes and peanut butter, washing it down with an orange-flavored Fuzzwonker Fizz. After a respectable eleven-second burp that could be heard all the way out on the street, I looked at the clock.

I'd only left Floyd alone for nine minutes, but it had seemed like a lot longer.

"I'll go check on him. See how he's doing," I said to myself.

When I arrived in Fizzopolis, my dad was waiting for me. "I was coming up to find you."

"How's Floyd doing?" I asked.

Dr. Fuzzwonker moved out of the path of the door and turned toward the open expanse of Fizzopolis.

"He might have missed you."

Floyd was bouncing all over the place, fast as a laser beam, breaking everything he banged into. Bottles of Fuzzwonker Fizz were flying everywhere. The conveyor belts were spinning out of control. Fizzies were running for their lives!

"Floyd!" I yelled.

Floyd heard my voice and stopped on a dime, hanging from the ceiling overhead. His eyes got big and excited.

"Better run for cover," I said. "This isn't going to be pretty."

Dr. Fuzzwonker nodded, moved three paces to the left, and put his hands in the pockets of his white mad-scientist lab coat.

Floyd zoomed through the air like an arrow shot from a crossbow! He landed on my face, and together we tumbled end over end.

When I sat up, Floyd was on my shoulder, whispering in my ear.

"What'd he say?" Dr. Fuzzwonker asked.

"He missed me."

Dr. Fuzzwonker nodded. "As I suspected."

I looked at Fizzopolis. The place was a *mess*.

I didn't know what to do. Neither did Dr. Fuzzwonker. It seemed like an impossible problem to solve, even for a food-mad scientist and a talented ten-year-old helper.

"I don't think we can keep you home from the fourth grade," Dr. Fuzzwonker said. "You'll have to go to school one way or another."

Floyd said something else into my ear, and I shook my head. Then Floyd put his whole arm inside my ear, which didn't feel great.

"Floyd thinks I should take him to school with me," I said.

Dr. Fuzzwonker looked at us both. "Outrageous!"

Floyd yanked my ear closer to his head.

"He says he'll be as quiet as a mouse. And he'll stay in my backpack at all times. We can handle it, Dad. No problem!"

Dr. Fuzzwonker looked at Fizzopolis. It was in bad shape.

"Are you absolutely positively sure beyond a shadow of a doubt you can keep Floyd a secret?"

I didn't think that was remotely possible, but I looked at Floyd, who was standing on my shoulder, and couldn't bring myself to let my little buddy down.

"We can do it."

"You'll need to be extra careful around Garvin Snood," Dr. Fuzzwonker said.

Garvin Snood. My archenemy! Garvin was Mr. Snood's son, and Mr. Snood owned the Snood Candy Factory. They made crummy candy at the other end of town in a weird factory. The Snoods were constantly searching for the secret Fuzzwonker Fizz recipe. And their head spy, Garvin Snood, would be in my fourth-grade class. It was going to be tricky keeping Floyd a secret.

Dr. Fuzzwonker nodded and began walking back to his laboratory.

"Let's get this place back into tip-top shape, shall we?"

"Will do!" I said.

Thinking about school the next day, I was about as nervous as I'd ever been, especially as I listened to the questions Floyd was asking.

"What will I wear? Who's this Snood character? What's the teacher's name? Have you got any extra pens? And paper. I'm going to need paper. And pants!"

CHAPTER 6

So now you know who's been drawing all over my journal—it's my best good buddy Floyd!

He even went back and drew all over the pages that were there before he started stowing away in my backpack. So now it's *our* journal of every adventure we have together. Best. Journal. Ever!

Monday morning I rode my red bike to Pflugerville Elementary School with my usual reckless abandon. I arrived at the bike racks about twelve seconds before the bell went off.

There's Floyd, peeking out of my backpack. This is an incredible day for him. It's the first day of school in his entire life. And there's the Snood Candy Factory off in the distance. See it? It's that lame-wad building with the smokestacks and the word SNOOD on it.

The Snoods only make one thing. It's called Flooze, but they package and shape Flooze into about a million different products. There are Flooze ropes, Flooze bars, Flooze gum, Flooze fake teeth, Flooze rings, Flooze juice, and a lot of Floozy things in brightly colored packaging. Every single Flooze product tastes like a gloppy ball of sugar at the bottom of a cereal bowl.

And like I said before, the Snoods are dying to get their hands on the secret recipe for Fuzz-wonker Fizz. Which is why it's so important they never find out about Floyd or the Fizzomatic machine. If they found out about the Fizzies and everything else going on under our house— whoa!—that would be a fizzy-sized catastrophe.

It turns out a lot can go wrong on the first day of school, especially if you're four inches tall, you're green, and you're confined to a backpack. It gets dull as dirt fast in a back-pack. Just ask your books, they'll tell you. It's a real snooze in there. Besides drawing all over my awesome journal, there's not much for Floyd to do. So Floyd said exactly what you'd expect him to say about five seconds after I sat down at my desk.

"It's boring in here. I ate my waffle. I'm thirsty. I'm so bored. Boooooored."

He repeated these things several times, but Floyd has a very small voice. He could scream and burp like a champ, but his voice was tiny. That's probably why he likes sitting on my shoulder so much. From there, his head lines right up with my ear.

I couldn't hear Floyd talking about how bored he was in my backpack, but he told me about it later.

Luckily for Floyd, he had packed a ball of rubber bands for situations like this one. He peeled open the backpack flap, loaded a rubber band in his stumpy little finger, and fired.

It missed me by a mile and hit Garvin Snood in the nose instead.

"HEY!" Garvin said. "What's the big idea, Fuzzwonker?"

"Huh?" I said.

HA Garvin had a gigantic nose, so it wasn't all that surprising that it had gotten in the way of Floyd's rubber band.

Garvin leaned closer to me.

"You better watch it, bub. I've got my eye on you."

The girl sitting on the other side of me, who was new at the school, piped in.

"Who you callin' bub, bub?"

It was the same girl who had cheered me on when I jumped my dad's car and face-planted with a milk shake.

What a disaster! The new kid and the Snood family candy spy in a fight. And I was sitting between them. I was attracting way too much attention.

"Zip it, newbie," Garvin Snood said to the girl.

"The name is Sammy, not newbie," she said.

"Figure it out, GLarvin."

I laughed. Garvin glared at me. He glared at Sammy. And then another rubber band hit him in the nose.

"FUZZWONKER!" Garvin yelled, holding his hand over his face.

"Now, boys," the teacher said. It was Miss Yoobler. She had also been my third-grade teacher. She had moved up to the fourth grade with me just like a student at the school, so I knew what to expect. Miss Yoobler was usually nice but sometimes not so much. She was especially not-so-much-nice when boys goofed off in class.

"He shot me in the face with a rubber band!" Garvin said.

"He did not!" Sammy said. "I was sitting right here. You shot *yourself* in the face with a rubber band!"

"That's not even possible!" Garvin said.

"Garvin," Miss Yoobler said. "Sammy is new. Be nice. And stop shooting yourself in the face with rubber bands. It's disrupting the class."

"But . . ."

Miss Yoobler put one finger in the air, a sign that she meant business. She took three steps toward Garvin and held her hand out. Sammy jumped up, collected the two rubber bands, and handed them to Miss Yoobler.

From his hiding spot, Floyd watched Miss Yoobler put his rubber bands into a box on her desk. It was a good-sized box, like a

 double-wide toaster. Miss Yoobler called it the misfit box.

It was full of all the things kids were not supposed to bring to school. I looked down and saw that Floyd was peeking out of my backpack, looking at the box, his eyes two little slits.

"Now, class," Miss Yoobler said, and then she turned to the whiteboard and started writing out a math problem with a red pen. "Let's pay attention or we'll never make it to the fifth grade! You'll be stuck here forever. Eyes this-a-way."

Garvin Snood leaned toward me and said, "This ain't over, Fuzzwonker."

Miss Yoobler's voice sounded like a hair dryer blasting information across the room. It seemed like a good time to check on Floyd, so I leaned over and pulled the flap on my backpack. I peered inside. It was kind of dark in there, but there was one thing that was 100 percent for sure not in the backpack.

Floyd.

Sammy saw Floyd at the same time I did. He was working his way under desks like a secret agent.

He looked like a real idiot, but he was having a very good time. Sammy could tell I was in trouble and bolted into action before I could stop her.

"Look!" she said, pointing to the window facing the playground. "It's a monkey!"

Everyone in class turned to the window.

"Where?" Miss Yoobler asked.

"Right there!" Sammy said, pointing as hard as she could.

Floyd saw his moment and ran out from under Jeff Flasky's desk. He zoomed to the front of the class, bounced off the wall, and landed on Miss Yoobler's desk. Then he slowly lifted the lid on the misfit box and jumped inside. It closed with a bang.

Miss Yoobler heard the box shut and turned with a confused look on her face.

Then she looked at the class.

"There are no monkeys at this school, I assure you," she said.

"I guess it was a very hairy teacher," Sammy said. "Sorry. I thought it was a monkey."

Garvin was on full alert. I was sure his dad, Mr. Snood, had already told him this was the

year. This was it! The fourth grade was the year that the Snoods would finally discover the secret recipe for Fuzzwonker Fizz. Garvin's sneaky spy brain was running through the situation: rubber bands being shot out of nowhere, monkey sightings, and the sound of Miss Yoobler's misfit box shutting on its own. Maybe it was all connected to the Fuzzwonker secret. There was certainly *something* going on. I had to be super-extra-double careful.

"Weird lizard you got there," Sammy said, leaning in toward me. "Does it bite?"

Red alert! Red alert! I thought. My hands started sweating.

"He's over there," Sammy said. "In that box on Miss Yoobler's desk. He's fast!"

"I know!" I whispered.

"He took off when the monkey showed up."

I turned to my left and saw that Garvin was staring at me.

"What are you up to, Fuzzwonker?"

Floyd told me later on that he was having the time of his life inside the misfit box. Miss Yoobler had been putting things in there since dinosaurs roamed the earth. She carried it from class to class. There were two comic books, a Slinky, a yo-yo, and three toy cars inside. And a squirt gun. Also a bottle of grape-flavored Fuzzwonker Fizz. Plus two rubber bands. There wasn't a lot of room to play, but there was just enough light seeping in through the cracks in the box so Floyd could kick back and read superhero stories.

"We need to get your lizard back, huh?" Sammy asked.

"Um, yeah. My *lizard*. Should we try the monkey again?"

"Nah. I have a better idea," Sammy said. Then she smiled and stood up.

CHAPTER 7

Sammy spoke in a slow, sleepy voice.

"I think my bear is in the gumball machine. Over at the milk shake shack! How'd you get in there, silly bear?"

Miss Yoobler turned around as Sammy moved like a zombie toward the back of the room.

"What's up with the weirdo?" Garvin asked.

"No one get near her!" Miss Yoobler said. "She must be sleepwalking! We must handle this carefully, kids. It's a delicate situation."

"Let's throw water in her face!" Garvin said.

"Garvin Snood, zip it," Miss Yoobler said.

Everyone watched Sammy as she zombie-walked, talking gibberish. "Come on, little bear, you've had enough cotton candy for one day. We need to brush your teeth and drive a hamburger before Mom gets home!"

"She's loopier than loopy," Garvin said.

Miss Yoobler walked past my desk and followed Sammy, which was my big chance to get Floyd out of the misfit box. I was up in a flash.

"Where do you think you're going?" Garvin asked, putting his foot out just as I went by. I tripped, wobbled, and pitched forward onto Miss Yoobler's desk. Garvin laughed so hard he snorted like a pig.

I opened the misfit box and found Floyd finishing off the bottle of grape-flavored Fuzz-wonker Fizz.

"Oh no," I said.

My back was to the class, so I grabbed Floyd and put my hand over his mouth. His eyes were getting bigger and bigger. He really needed to burp.

"It's okay," Miss Yoobler said, standing next to Sammy. "My dog is also a sleepwalker. I have experience with this sort of thing. You're going to be fine."

"How am I going to get you out of that gumball machine?" Sammy asked in a sleepy voice. "I know! I'll hit it with a hammer!"

"I'm going to clap three times fast," Miss Yoobler said. "And when I do, you will be wide-awake."

"Slap the gumball machine three times with a blender," Sammy said. "Why didn't *I* think of that?"

Miss Yoobler clapped three times fast.

Floyd loaded up a rubber band he'd picked

up in the misfit box and pointed it at me. I blocked him with my hand, and that meant there was nothing covering his mouth anymore.

My back was to the class when Sammy woke up. "Did someone see a monkey? I thought I saw a monkey."

Then I heard Miss Yoobler. "Mr. Fuzzwonker! Get back to your desk this instant!"

Floyd's stomach had expanded to about three times its normal size.

"You gotta be kidding me," I said.

"Harold! Did you hear what I said?" Miss Yoobler boomed.

Teacher: BLAH BLAH BLAH BLAH

BLAH BLAH

BLAH

And that was when Floyd let loose with a huge Fuzz-wonker Fizz burp.

"BBBRRRAAAAAAAAAAAOOOOEEE—"
The room shook like an earthquake had just struck.

"EEEAAAAAAARRRRR—" RRRRRRRR
A picture fell off the wall.

RRRUU "UUUUAAARRRCCHHHRRRAAAU-
UUUUUUGGGGHHHH!"
Finally, after sixteen seconds, Floyd's burp

ended. I was facing away from the class, so they all thought it was me. He smiled happily and I stuffed him in my pocket. The class cheered and laughed.

"Everyone back to your desks! We've got math to learn!" Miss Yoobler said.

Garvin watched me like a hawk. It was another ten minutes before I could safely transfer Floyd from my pocket to my backpack. I made a mental note to bring comic books the next day so Floyd would have something to do. And to never, ever—under any circumstances—bring Fuzzwonker Fizz to school.

CHAPTER 8

After school, Garvin followed me toward the bike rack. He was careful to stay out of sight, hiding behind large objects like trash cans and teachers, but I saw him.

I cut between a gaggle of students and ducked into a classroom.

"Let's wait here for a second and make sure he doesn't try to follow us home," I said.

Floyd poked his head out of my backpack, and the flap hung over his head like a fedora.

I could hear his small voice

from there, but all he did was ask if I could have a pizza delivered to my backpack.

"No way," I said. "You'll get cheese all over my books. We'll be back in Fizzopolis before you know it. You can eat then."

Floyd complained about being hungry and shut the flap. I could hear him using a marker in there, making grumbling noises as he scribbled all over my journal.

I had been super-extremely-tremendously careful not to take my backpack off for the rest of the day. Wearing it was best, because:

a) I wouldn't leave it on the playground by accident (I have done that about ten million times).

b) Floyd could ask me things like "When's lunch?" and I could hear him.

c) Garvin Snood couldn't get his grubby hands on my backpack if I was wearing it.

I arrived at my bike and looked every which way.

"No sign of Garvin," I said. "Must have lost him. I'm going to set you on the ground for just a second while I unlock my bike."

I set the bag down while Floyd asked me what the thing on a stick was they'd served in the cafeteria for lunch and when could he make some in Fizzopolis because he was sure all the Fizzies would like whatever it was.

"It was a corn dog, silly," I said. "You really need to get out more."

When I turned to grab my backpack, Garvin rode by on his mountain bike and snatched it.

"Hey!" I said.

"Hey is for losers, loser!" Garvin laughed. Garvin's bike was way, way too big for a fourth grader, and he swerved back and forth down the sidewalk like a total dork. But it was a fast bike with lots of gears. He was wearing my backpack on one shoulder and his own on the other. And he was getting away with the Fuzz-wonker family trust!

Sammy raced by on her green bike with the banana seat and the sissy bar.

"Come on! We gotta get your lizard back!"

I was on my bike in nothing flat, pedaling like a maniac. If there was one thing I was good at, it was riding my red bike. I raced all the way even with Sammy, but we weren't gaining on Snood yet.

"Say, you're fast!" Sammy said. "But can you do this?"

Sammy turned sharp to the right, hopped the curb, and rode right through a front yard, cutting the corner and gaining on Snood. I followed right behind, taking the curb and the yard, no problem.

"Nice move back there," I said. "We're gaining on him!"

We pedaled on, faster and faster, until we came to the curvy stretch of the neighborhood. Garvin wobbled like crazy as he made the turns, and Floyd was leaning out of my backpack, looking inside Garvin's backpack. I could tell my little buddy was thinking about jumping.

"Stay put, Floyd!" I yelled.

"Who's Floyd?" Sammy asked.

"I'll tell you later. Follow me!"

I weaved off the road and dodged the trees lining the sidewalk with Sammy close behind. It was straighter in the front yards, and we came even with Garvin, who was barely holding it together on the turns.

"I have an idea!" Sammy said. "Here, take one of these. Uncork it!"

"I can't believe you eat this stuff," I said. Sammy had a tube of Snood's Flooze in her hand, the yuckiest candy on earth.

"I don't eat it," Sammy said. "I use it for gluing macaroni to cardboard and fixing the sole of my shoe when it comes unstuck at the toe."

The Snood's Flooze she had was packaged like a tube of toothpaste. I heard it tasted like a bowl of flour soaked in syrup, but that was just a rumor because I'd never tried it.

"Come on! We're ahead!" Sammy said.

She turned sharp for the sidewalk, bunny-hopped over a stray cat, and narrowly avoided

83

a mailbox before entering the street in front of Garvin.

"Start squirting!" she yelled. I followed Sammy over the cat and around the mailbox and pointed the tube of Snood's Flooze behind me. Then I squeezed the tube as hard as I could.

Sammy did the same, filling the road with a sticky coat of Flooze. When Garvin's tires hit the Flooze, his bike started to slow down.

We slammed on our brakes and waited. Garvin's wheels were covered in Snood's Flooze, and the tires were sticking to the pavement. By the time he cleared the pool of Flooze, Garvin's tires were soaked in sticky sludge. It got to

MAIL

where he was pedaling as hard as he could, but he was barely moving. An old lady with a walker passed him on the sidewalk.

I pulled up along one side, and Sammy

pulled up on the other. We leisurely rode with no hands and had a little conversation.

"Nice day, right?" I said.

"Not bad. I could do with a little rain," Sammy said. "Big fan of rain."

Garvin was pouring sweat. He pedaled harder than he'd ever pedaled in his life.

Finally, when he was so winded he couldn't even speak, he pulled his bike over to the sidewalk and flopped over like a dead fish.

"Here you go," Sammy said, picking up my backpack and handing it to me.

"Thanks!" I said.

"I just hope your lizard is okay."

Garvin started to catch his breath and sat up as we rode away.

"FUZZWONKEEEEEEEEEEER!"

When we were safely down the street, I decided to check on Floyd. I stopped, opened the backpack, and searched inside. I moved all my books back and forth. I pulled this journal out. I turned it over and dumped everything onto somebody's front yard.

"This is impossible!" I screamed.

Sammy looked at me like I was losing my marbles, but this was about as big a deal as big deals get.

Floyd was not in my backpack.

CHAPTER
9,000,00

I made a fateful decision then. I decided to let Sammy in on the Fuzzwonker family trust. Taking Floyd to school was going to be harder than I thought. If today had been a sample of days to come, there was no way I could hide Floyd from sneaky Garvin all by myself. I needed a friend.

"Floyd is not a lizard," I said.

"You mean the little green guy who lives in your backpack?" Sammy asked. "I wondered about that."

I put everything back into my backpack,

and we started riding to where we'd peeled off from Garvin. While we rode, I told Sammy everything. I used my super-fast voice because that's the voice I use when I'm worried. And boy was I worried. I gave her the entire story of Fizzopolis in one breath.

"So that's where Floyd came from?" Sammy asked.

"Yeah, that's where Floyd came from. He got attached to me and when I'd leave, he sort of—"

"Freaked out?" Sammy suggested.

"Yeah. He can be a troublemaker."

"You don't say?"

"But he's my best good buddy! I have to take care of him. I wasn't supposed to tell anyone about Fizzopolis or Floyd. But I need a friend. This is a really big responsibility."

We arrived where Garvin had been, but he was gone. And there was no sign of Floyd.

"Say no more," Sammy said. "If Floyd is your best good buddy, then I'll be your super-duper palomino."

I nodded because having a super-duper pal-omino sounded like something every person should be lucky enough to have.

"There's one more thing," I said. "The Snoods are serious trouble. They've been trying to steal the Fuzzwonker Fizz recipe for-ever, so Garvin is always spying on me. If he has Floyd, he's going to wonder where my best good buddy came from. It's going to get ugly."

"Well, he's nowhere around here," Sammy said. "Are you sure he stayed in your back-pack?"

I thought about chasing Garvin Snood, and that's when I remembered Floyd peeking into Garvin's backpack. He must have seen some-thing he liked in there.

"He's in Garvin's backpack!" I yelled.

Sammy spun a wheelie on her bike and rode around in a circle. When she landed her front wheel, she stopped.

"Then we better follow this."

Sure enough, there was a trail of goopy

Snood's Flooze from Garvin's bike tires.

And looking off in the distance, I saw that it seemed to be leading to the far end of town.

"The Snood Candy Factory!" I yelled.

"Come on, super-duper palomino," Sammy said. "Let's go get your best good buddy back."

CHAPTER 10

Don't Come in Here!

BEWARE OF DOGS!

PRIVATE PROPERTY!

Garvin was obviously winded on his way to the Snood Candy Factory because the trail wobbled back and forth and looped all over the place. There was a winding hill of a driveway at the bottom of the Snood property, and here it appeared that he'd taken a break and leaned his bike against a gnarly old tree. There were signs everywhere: BEWARE OF DOGS! DON'T COME IN HERE! PRIVATE PROPERTY!

"Looks like he stopped here," Sammy said.

A couple of squirrels stared at us from the

limbs of the tree, but I didn't see Floyd up there. I didn't see Floyd *anywhere*.

"Let's keep going," I said. "But stay quiet. By the looks of these signs, they have guard dogs."

"I like dogs," Sammy said. "I hope you're right."

I didn't think these would be the kind of dogs Sammy would like. If the Snoods did have guard dogs, they'd be the kind with big barks and bigger teeth.

We took it slow and soon the narrow road was covered with a canopy of tangled tree limbs. They hid us from the sun, but little shafts of light broke through. We went through a long covered bridge that was even darker inside. A sludgy stream ran under the bridge.

"The Snoods really know how to make a girl feel welcome," Sammy said.

"Shhhhh. They probably have this place wired."

Sammy looked at me and all I could see were

the whites of her eyes. "You're being paranoid. It's not like they're watching us or anything."

Right after Sammy said that, a huge voice boomed and echoed through the covered bridge.

"WHO DARES ENTER THE PRIVATE PROPERTY OF THE SNOODS WITHOUT PERMISSION?" I felt like the Wizard of Oz was yelling down at me.

"Come on!" Sammy said. "It's only a little farther!"

I raced out in front and we cleared the other side of the covered bridge. The Snood Candy Factory loomed up before us, dark and forbidding. It was tall and square with billowing smokestacks and one set of big doors. There were windows along the walls, but they were all too high up for us to look through.

"There!" I said.

Sammy saw it, too. Floyd stared down at us from one of the windows. With a smile on his face, he was eating a glob of Snood's Flooze.

I waved for him to come out, but he just pointed to the Snood's Flooze like he couldn't believe how much free candy there was inside the factory.

"He's not going to come out on his own," I said. "We'll have to go in and get him."

We rode to the far side of the factory and leaned our bikes against the brick wall.

"DON'T MAKE ME SEND OUT THE DOGS!" the voice boomed again.

"That must be Mr. Snood yelling," I said. "He doesn't come out. Ever. He just stays in there and makes lousy Floozy candy."

"I hope he sends the dogs," Sammy said. "I love dogs."

"Sammy, I don't think you're going to like these ones."

"Of course I will. Why wouldn't I?"

I looked down the long wall of the Snood

Candy Factory. It was nothing but bricks and locked doors and windows—nowhere we could sneak in.

"Come on, let's try going around the back of the building," I said.

We left the bikes behind and quietly tiptoed to the edge of the factory. There were more trees back there, lots of them. And we found a little door. It was only about two feet tall.

"There's no handle on this weird door," Sammy said as she stepped closer.

"I have a bad feeling about this," I said. "I don't think that's a door for people."

Mr. Snood's voice blared into the forest behind the factory again. "DON'T SAY I DIDN'T WARN YOU!"

And then the door opened up. Sammy leaned her head inside like it was no big deal. Then she looked at me.

"It's dark in there. Like *really* dark."

I peered inside with her and wished I'd brought a flashlight.

"Do you hear that?" I asked.

"Hear what?"

It sounded like a couple of Rottweilers running through a dark passageway toward two kids poking their heads through a small door.

"RUN!" I yelled at the top of my lungs. I didn't have to tell myself twice. I have a mortal fear of being chased by giant dogs. It happened to me once on my paper route. There I was, just minding my own business and trying to earn a few extra bucks, when a dog the size of a hippopotamus started chasing me down the street. It bit the heel right off my brand-new pair of high-tops. I have half a shoe to prove it.

I was all the way to the farthest end of the Snood Candy Factory when I finally turned back. Sammy wasn't anywhere in sight. She hadn't followed me. Or she *had* followed and the dogs had grabbed her and dragged her out

into the woods like a play toy!

What I wanted to do was run for my bike and hightail it for home, but there was no way I could leave both my super-duper palomino *and* my best good buddy behind. So I slowly walked back toward the small door. I used my softest footsteps, but it didn't matter. There were a lot of dead leaves and twigs on the ground, and it was impossible to miss them all.

"Sammy?" I whispered. She didn't answer, so I

kept going until I was back at the door, staring inside. I said Sammy's name again and my
voice echoed softly, dying about two feet into
the darkness.

"Whatcha doin', super-duper palomino?"

I jumped four feet into the air, did three
flips, and landed on my butt. There was also
some screaming.

"Don't sneak up on me like that!" I said. "I
almost had a heart attack!"

Sammy was standing between two ginor-
mous dogs. Their heads were the size of
prize-winning pumpkins.

And the teeth! They were bigger than my whole arm! Okay, not that big. But they were still huge. Both dogs had slobbery sticks in their mouths. Sammy patted them on their heads, took the sticks, and chucked them behind her.

"I love dogs," she said as the dogs tore off into the woods behind the factory.

I brushed all the nature off my butt and stood up. "Sammy, you are incredible."

Sammy crouched down in front of the doggy door and peered inside. "We could go this way. Whaddaya say?"

"I say sure. And let's close the door behind us. The dogs probably want to stay out and play awhile."

"Good plan."

We crept into the darkness and closed the doggy door. The passageway wound around like a garden hose, but after a while, we could see some light.

"I think we might have just made it inside the Snood Candy Factory," I said.

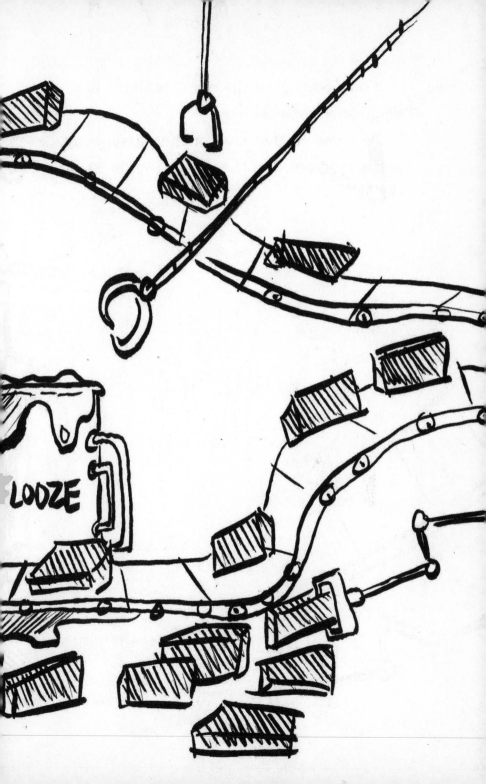

"Cool," Sammy whispered. "I wish the dogs could have come with us."

We came to the edge of the passageway and stared out into the wacky weirdness of the factory.

CHAPTER
11

The Snood Candy Factory was cast in yellow and orange light, and there were giant vats with squishy green gross stuff sloshing over the edges. Conveyer belts rolled all over the place and made squeaky sounds like they needed oiling. They carried slabs of Snood's Flooze that looked like blocks of gray bubble gum. There were robot arms grabbing the Flooze, wrapping them in colorful packaging, and stuffing them in boxes.

"Hey, isn't that your little buddy up there?" Sammy said.

She pointed to one of the conveyer belts, where Floyd held two bars of Flooze, biting into them one at a time like chicken legs. He was being carried up and up into the top section of the factory. I followed the long line of the conveyor belt to see where it was headed. It looked like it would reach a high point and then slant downward toward a wrapping station.

"My best good buddy is about to get packaged and shipped!" I said. "We gotta move fast."

I took a mental picture of the whole place, including: Mr. Snood, standing on a catwalk way over our heads. There were all sorts of knobs, levers, and buttons in front of him. There was also a big horn that extended out into the middle of the factory like a snake with a king-sized round head. Mr. Snood controlled everything, moving back and forth at lightning speed.

Several alarms sounded all around him, and he was obviously distracted.

Garvin Snood was sitting in a corner of the factory, leaning back on a chair, reading a comic book. He looked like he was about to fall asleep.

Floyd was getting dangerously close to the top of the conveyor belt and heading down toward the packaging station.

"Garvin!" Mr. Snood bellowed into the horn. "Stop

FLOOZE VAT

reading that comic book and let the dogs back in! Those kids must have run off."

Mr. Snood laughed maniacally, like he was really happy he'd chased off a couple of Pflugerville's finest. Shaped like a pear in his white sci- entist coat, he was splattered with Flooze. He looked like a much older ver- sion of Garvin: big nose, round eyes, and a shock of dark hair.

"Come on, Dad," Garvin complained. "Let 'em chase that dumb Fuzzwonker kid awhile longer. It makes me happy."

"Garvin!" Mr. Snood yelled.

Garvin got up like a sloth. "Okay, okay. I'm going already."

That was when I noticed the last and possibly most important thing of all. Next to the opening of the passageway, there was a button that said *Doggy Door.*

"Can you control those two monsters?" I asked Sammy.

"You mean the dogs? Sure I can. Easy."

I nodded, reached my hand into the factory, and slammed my hand down on the button. Sammy whistled behind me, but the factory was so loud Mr. Snood didn't hear her. She had a good aim with her whistle, and it flew down the long tube until it reached the dogs. A few seconds later, I could hear them racing toward us, barking and banging into the walls as they each tried to take the lead.

"There goes Garvin," I said. He'd reached the only doors into the place and unlatched the lock.

"I've got the dogs ready," Sammy said. "What do you want them to do?"

I turned around and both dogs licked my face. Each tongue, I'm telling you, was like the size of a wet tennis shoe.

I wiped all the slobber off my face.

"We need a diversion," I said.

"Got it!" she said. Sammy turned to the dogs and spoke to them like they were her children.

Floyd had reached the top of the conveyor belt and he was heading down, right toward the robot arms and the packaging!

"Off you go," Sammy said, and both dogs took off at a run into the factory.

The dogs ran up a long flight of metal stairs and arrived at the control tower for the factory. They showered Mr. Snood with affection, which included leaping up into his face and barking with reckless abandon.

"Follow me!" I said.

I ran farther into the factory, ducking to avoid low-hanging beams and conveyor belts and leaning around robot arms. I leaped onto a conveyor belt heading up and started running to the top with Sammy close behind.

"Uh, Harold?" Sammy said behind me.

"Yeah?"

"Garvin is back."

From the top of the factory I saw the door opening and Garvin walked in.

"Get these dogs off me!" Mr. Snood yelled into the horn.

"Oh, hey, you found them," Garvin said. "Way to go, Dad."

Garvin headed up the stairs toward the dogs, and I jumped onto the conveyer belt Floyd was on. He was way down at the bottom, eating Flooze without a care in the world.

"Here we go," I said, and then I rode that

conveyor belt like a snowboard. Snood's
Flooze bars flew everywhere and a new alarm
sounded.

Sammy was right behind me, sliding fast,
and we were on a crash course with Floyd at
the bottom.

"GET THOSE KIDS OUT OF MY FACTORY!"
Mr. Snood yelled into the horn.

Garvin jumped on a conveyor belt of his
own, sliding down toward us. Floyd had
reached the packaging area. The robot arms
wrapped him up tight in a Flooze package and
sent him down the line toward the boxes.

"Prepare for impact!" I yelled.

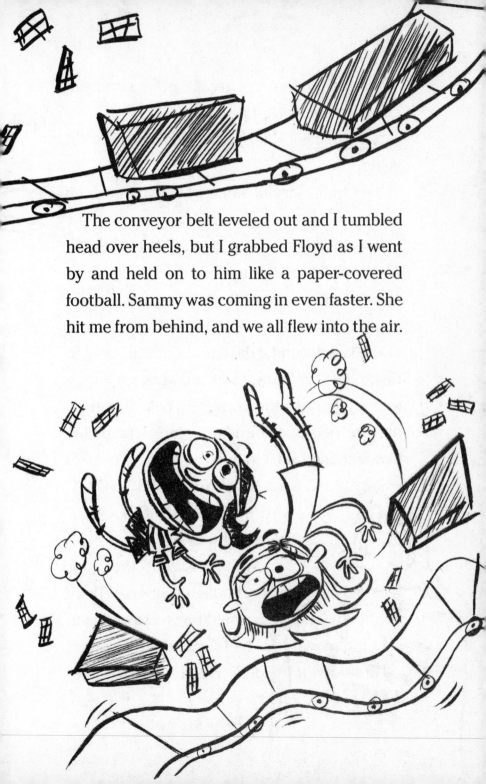

The conveyor belt leveled out and I tumbled head over heels, but I grabbed Floyd as I went by and held on to him like a paper-covered football. Sammy was coming in even faster. She hit me from behind, and we all flew into the air.

Our landing was not great, but we survived, and then we started running.

"Come back here, Fuzzwonker!" Garvin yelled.

"Get him, Garvin!" Mr. Snood said into the horn.

Garvin was over our heads on one of the conveyor belts, and he attempted a very complicated dive from one belt to another. He was about to tackle me like a fumbled football, but at the last second, I darted out of the way. Little did Garvin know, I was standing on a very bouncy part of the conveyor belt. When he hit, the belt buckled like a giant trampoline and launched Garvin into the air.

"AAAAAAYYYYYOOOOOAA-AAAAAAYYYYAAAAOOOOOO!" he screamed.

We arrived at the door and pulled it open. When I turned back, I saw Garvin had landed in a vat of Flooze. He bobbed up

114

and down, covered in marshmallow cream.

"Fuzzwonker!" Garvin yelled, only it sounded like he had a mouthful of taffy.

"OUT!" Mr. Snood roared. And then the dogs jumped up and licked his face again.

"No problem, sir," I said. "Sorry for the interruption."

We bolted out the door and sprinted to our bikes. I've never pedaled that fast in my life. We pedaled so fast I thought my legs were going to start smoking from the friction.

When we were safely away, we pulled over on the sidewalk and Sammy held our wrapped-up tiny buddy. I tore the paper away and found Floyd fast asleep, his goofy little mouth covered in Flooze.

"I guess he overdid it," Sammy said.

"The first day of school will do that to a guy," I agreed. "Put him in my backpack, will ya?"

Sammy carefully set Floyd in my backpack, and I could hear him snoring lightly as we started off again.

I thought about what to do. Dr. Fuzzwonker wouldn't give me a dinosaur for two more years. I wasn't going to drive the car or get a flying motorcycle anytime soon. But maybe I'd get a yes if I asked for a sidekick.

"Come on," I said. "Let's go talk to my dad."

CHAPTER 12

"So, how did it go?" Dr. Fuzzwonker asked when I showed up at home a half hour later. We took the elevator down to Fizzopolis.

"It was mostly average, I guess. I learned some math."

"Well, that's just fabulous, isn't it? And how about our little friend? How did *he* do?"

"Oh, Floyd did fine," I said. "He was no trouble at all."

"Marvelous!" Dr. Fuzzwonker said.

I stepped out of the elevator and let the doors close.

"Um, Dad?"

Dr. Fuzzwonker headed for his tree-house laboratory, so he didn't notice that the elevator had gone back upstairs, where it would pick up Sammy.

"It's not as easy as I thought it might be keeping Floyd a secret."

Dr. Fuzzwonker gasped. "Did Garvin Snood see him? Say it isn't so!"

"I kept him safe from the Snoods."

"*WHEW!* You had me worried there for a second."

Floyd sat on my shoulder and yawned. When I turned around and saw that the elevator had reached the kitchen, I knew I was running out of time. I'd given Sammy specific instructions about how to use the elevator, and now she was coming down. Better spill the beans.

All in one breath, I asked: "I know I can't have a dinosaur yet or drive the car or ride a flying motorcycle, but if it's okay with you, I could really, really, really use a sidekick with

Floyd sat down on the Ping-Pong table and began interviewing for the position of travel buddy. Every Fizzy in Fizzopolis lined up.

"Son," Dr. Fuzzwonker said. "I think we've created a monster."

Dr. Fuzzwonker didn't know the half of it!

In that same week, Floyd jumped into a vat of macaroni and cheese in the school lunchroom.

A week after that, he tried to put on a talent show in Fizzopolis, because they had one at my school. He organized an escape on Halloween and took all the Fizzies trick-or-treating.

Sammy and I were only getting started at the tasks of keeping Floyd out of trouble, guarding the recipe for Fuzzwonker Fizz, and protecting the biggest secret in the world.

Fizzopolis!

The night after Floyd's first day at school, I woke up and found him sleeping on the windowsill.

"What the heck are you doing out of bed?" I asked.

Floyd didn't answer. He was too busy snoring and probably dreaming about the Snood Candy Factory and what was inside. I'm pretty sure he was also thinking about running through the

neighborhood in his underpants and sneaking into the building so he could eat Flooze all night.

Because there is a secret among Fizzies that only Fizzies know. Well, a secret only Fizzies and *me* know. Floyd told me.

For Fizzies, Flooze is the best-tasting candy on earth. They live for that stuff!

Sammy and I might think it's about the crummiest candy there ever was, but Floyd and his Fizzy buddies love Flooze.

As I looked out the window, I could imagine Mr. Snood in the Snood Candy Factory. He was probably saying something like this: "I must have that Fuzzwonker Fizz recipe! It's worth millions! Billions! Zillions!"

From where Mr. Snood stood, he could see Flooze being pulled in giant goopy sheets, stretched, cut, and wrapped. All those squeaky gears, rolling conveyor belts, and robotic arms lifting boxes and boxes of Snood's Flooze. He probably just took a sloppy bite of grape-flavored Flooze and washed it down with a bottle of strawberry Fuzzwonker Fizz.

That Fuzzwonker Fizz is pure magic, a taste explosion that would have puckered his lips and sent chills down his spine. I bet he burped for seven seconds in a row, a dud by Fizz standards, then turned to the neighborhood outside.

"Fuzzwonker Fizz will be mine. All mine! Mine! Mine! Mine! Muahahahahahahahaha-hahahaaaaa!"

Or maybe he's asleep. How should I know?

124

Turn the page
for a sneak peek at

CHAPTER 1

I'm Harold Fuzzwonker and I'm sitting in my classroom, where Miss Yoobler is about to start a movie. Miss Yoobler has terrible taste in movies, and she never gives out popcorn. And she makes us take notes! Who takes notes during a movie?

"Now, class," Miss Yoobler droned. "*The History of Flour* is an informative and exciting documentary that will change the way you think about hot dog buns and pizza crust. Prepare to be moved."

The History of Flour was part four of a series

we were watching. These movies make me feel like my eyeballs are going to fall out and roll around like marbles on the classroom floor. We've already completed *The Story of a Chicken*, *Butter My Toast*, and *Super Cobs: The Amazing Journey of Corn*.

Miss ~~Yoobler~~ turned off the lights and started the movie. The screen filled with rows of swaying wheat and the sound of a tractor.

My best friend, Sammy, leaned slightly toward me and said, "I thought this movie was about pizza."

"And hot dogs," I added.

"You two are total airheads," Jeff Flasky said. Flasky had an enormous head and big, round eyes. He was also the smartest kid in class.

"What does a field full of whatever that

stuff is have to do with pepperoni pizza?" Sammy wondered. Flasky rolled his eyes as Miss Yoobler took three long strides toward us.

"Zip it, Fuzzwonker," Miss Yoobler said. She was the strictest teacher in the entire United States of America. Unfortunately, Sammy was in a talkative mood and she kept yammering about pizza and hot dogs. Miss Yoobler took three more steps and loomed over my left shoulder like Frankenstein.

Garvin Snood was sitting two desks over. He was always trying to figure out the secret of Fuzzwonker Fizz, so we had to be extra-super careful around him.

"You boneheads are in for it now," Garvin sniggered. He laughed like a hyena.

Miss Yoobler tapped her foot on the linoleum. It was like Chinese water torture.

"Harold Fuzzwonker, come with me," she finally said.

"Take me!" Sammy said. "I'll gladly go to the principal's office!

Last time I went there they had donuts and better movies."

I picked up my backpack and Miss Yoobler marched me to an empty desk in the farthest back corner of the class. Sammy waved at me with a faraway look like we were separated by a giant river filled with crocodiles.

"Let's see if sitting in Siberia will help you concentrate, Mr. Fuzzwonker," Miss Yoobler said. She stood next to me for a while, but then Garvin Snood threw a wad of paper at Jeff Flasky and hit him in the side of his huge head.

"Garvin!" Miss Yoobler yelled, and then she was on the move toward Garvin's desk.

I looked down at my backpack sitting on the floor. It was squirming wildly like a tennis ball was bouncing around inside. There were also muffled noises coming from under the flap.

"Oh, great," I said. I nudged the side of the bag with my foot and made a *shhhhhhhh* sound. For a second everything was calm, but then the whole bag rolled over on its side and

HA HA HA HA HA HA HA HA HA HA HA HA HA HA HA HA HA HA HA HA HA HA HA HA HA HA HA HA HA HA HA HA HA HA HA HA HA HA HA HA HA

flopped forward. I heard the sound of laughing in there.

"Calm down, little buddy!" I whispered. "I'm already in enough trouble as it is."

In case you don't know about my best good buddy who lives in my backpack, his name is Floyd. How he got there takes a little explaining, but since we're watching a mindless movie about flour, I can take a second to fill you in.

The super-short story of how Floyd got in my backpack, by me, Harold Fuzzwonker (sure to be more interesting than the History of Flour):

My dad is Dr. Fuzzwonker, and he keeps a top secret laboratory under our house. It's the biggest laboratory you've ever seen—like several football fields—because some of what my dad makes needs a lot of space to roam. He creates Fuzzwonker Fizz, the soda pop that produces the biggest burps in the world. It's extremely popular stuff that comes in about one hundred flavors. You should try some!

Classroom status update: I need to speed this up because Floyd is sucker punching me in the solar plexus. Ouch. I advise reading the next paragraph at double speed!

Dr. Fuzzwonker uses a machine he calls the Fizzomatic to make Fuzzwonker Fizz, but he also used it to make Floyd. Floyd is a Fizzy, and he's not the only one. There are at least a hundred different Fizzies in my dad's humongous secret space under the house, which is probably why he calls it Fizzopolis. Floyd just happens to be the smallest one and the biggest troublemaker.

And that's why he has to go with me in my backpack to school. If he stays in Fizzopolis without me, he misses me too much and that makes him go bonkers. He makes huge messes and causes colossal problems. So every day when I leave for school I carefully pack Floyd into my backpack and hope he stays quiet. This almost never happens, so I spend a lot of time struggling to keep Floyd a secret.

See how short that was! And trust me, you didn't miss anything important about flour. You're all good. I can't say the same for myself. While you've been busy reading all about Floyd, I've been freaking out.

My backpack was flopping toward the front of the class like a sack of potatoes rolling down a hill.

I couldn't yell at Floyd or everyone would hear me and ask me who Floyd is. I glanced toward the door, where Miss Yoobler had stationed herself. At first I thought she was staring down into her phone, probably texting some pro wrestler for advice about how to keep her class from disobeying her. But then I realized she'd fallen asleep and that gave me some extra courage.

I got down on all fours and started crawl-
ing as the bag moved toward the front of the
class.

I passed a couple of other kids who were
sound asleep, and then Jeff Flasky, who was
diligently taking notes. The next desk I was
going to pass would be Garvin's. Total disaster dead ahead.

The bag was getting dangerously close
to Garvin's mondo-sized foot, so I pulled a
pencil out from behind my ear and threw it
tomahawk-style at the back of Sammy's head.

Luckily, it hit her noggin eraser end first. Sammy is my super-duper palomino. She's the only other kid in the world that knows about Floyd.

Sammy turned in Garvin's direction and narrowed her eyes like a ninja ready to strike. But then she saw me, and I nodded toward the bag creeping across the floor. Her eyes darted from me to the backpack moving on its own, nearly at Garvin's feet. Then she stared at Garvin.

"What are you looking at, weirdo?" Garvin asked.

Sammy sprang into action. In a matter of less than 1.3 seconds, she did five things in rapid succession:

She reached into her own backpack, pulled out a bologna sandwich, and took it out of the Ziploc bag.

She jumped into the air and did a roundhouse kick that landed squarely on my backpack! The bag (and Floyd inside) slammed into my face and knocked me onto my back. Boy, she could really kick hard. When I sat up, I had my bag (and Floyd) in a bear hug.

When Sammy landed, she stared at Garvin like she was going to hurl. Garvin had a look on his face that screamed: *This kid is about to barf on me!*

Sammy made a really loud BLAAAAAA-GGGLAAAAAAAK sound and acted like she was throwing up all over Garvin.

She tossed her bologna sandwich at him and it bounced off of his massive forehead.

All the bread and bologna and lettuce came apart on his desk.

"AAAAAAAAAAUUAAAAAAUUU-AAAAAUUUUUUAAAAA!" Garvin screamed. He was sure he'd been thrown up on and *wow* was he freaking out about it. It didn't look like real barf. It looked like a bologna sandwich.

"Garvin stole my lunch!" Sammy yelled.

"Sammy barfed on me!" Garvin yelled.

The whole class went bananas.

There was a lot of laughing and shouting and running around the room.

"Order! Order, I say!" Miss Yoobler said. She stomped over to Garvin's desk like an army sergeant. While all the chaos was going on in the room, I crawled back to my desk in Siberia and tied a bunch of knots on the bag flap so Floyd couldn't escape, then I slung the pack on and cinched it down tight in case it tried to roll away again.

"She threw up on me!" Garvin said from the other end of the room. "On purpose!"

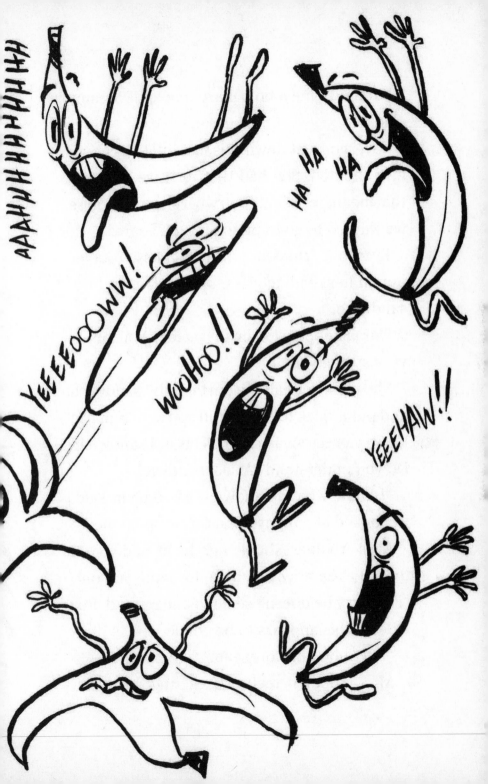

"You owe me a bologna sandwich!" Sammy said.

"Everyone sit down this instant!" Miss Yoobler shouted. She had that tone we all knew that meant we'd better do what she said unless we wanted to go to prison for ten years.

Everyone calmed down as Miss Yoobler put on her reading glasses and examined the sandwich.

"Mr. Snood," she finally said. "You are a very strange boy."

She picked up all the parts of the sandwich and put it back together and spoke to him like he was a very small child. "This is a sandwich. Do you understand? A saaaaandwich."

"I know what a sandwich is!" Garvin said. He looked at Sammy. "She threw up on me!"

Miss Yoobler shook her head sadly and looked at Sammy. She held the sandwich out. "I'm sorry he doesn't seem to understand. But at least this appears to be edible."

"It touched his forehead," Sammy said.

Miss Yoobler reeled back and held the

sandwich as far away from herself as she could. She marched over to the garbage can and dropped it inside.

The class settled down and we returned to watching *The History of Flour.*

Floyd started bashing into me from inside my backpack. It felt like he was doing barrel rolls into my rib cage, so I squashed him against the back of my seat.

When school finally let out, Sammy and I ran to our bikes. We had to get out of there fast and figure out what the heck was going on with my best good buddy.

"Where to?" Sammy asked as we started off.

There was only one place where

we could safely let Floyd out into the open. It was a place where no one from the outside world would see him.

"Fizzopolis!" I said, and we tore off into the neighborhood at triple speed.

CHAPTER 2

"Oooooh, look," I said when we arrived in the kitchen at my house. "Pancakes."

"Stand back. I'm hungry!" Sammy said. "Miss Yoobler threw my lunch away."

"Yeah, I saw that. Thanks again for saving my bacon."

"It cost me a bologna sandwich, but it was worth it."

There were nineteen pancakes in the stack (I counted them) and it teetered back and forth like a skyscraper in an earthquake. We took turns throwing them at each other like Frisbees and catching them in our mouths. Talk about a good time. I opened my backpack and dropped the last five inside, then cinched it tight again before Floyd could climb out.

"Come on, let's get into Fizzopolis where it's safe," I said.

"Will do, super-duper palomino," Sammy said. But she had a mouthful of pancake, so it came out like Fu fo, foofer foofer fafofifo.

We opened the refrigerator door and I leaned deep inside and found the hot sauce. I turned it like a lug nut.

"Hot SAWCE," I said slowly, and the refrigerator moved about three feet to one side.

"I love your house," Sammy said. She

reached down and picked up a nickel covered in dust bunnies and handed it to me.

"Thanks, I was looking for that," I said, and pushed a button on the wall.

"Remember the most important rule of Fizzopolis?" I asked.

Sammy nodded as the elevator doors opened.

"Don't tell anyone about all the cool stuff down there," Sammy said. "Got it!"

I handed Sammy a huge stick of bubble gum and put another stick in my mouth. We chewed and chewed until the gum was nice and gooey and then we threw both wads into the elevator. They hit the floor with a slobbery slap sound. We jumped into the elevator and made sure to land with one shoe each on a wad of gum so we

Fu Fo foofer foofer fafofifo

were good and stuck.

"Here we go!" I said, and I pressed the button for Fizzopolis.

It felt like I was skydiving without a parachute as we plummeted underground.

"I can't get enough of this elevator!" Sammy said. But then our feet slipped out of our shoes and we spent the rest of the trip stuck to the ceiling. Both of us tried to crawl down the side of the wall but only made it halfway before the elevator stopped. We fell face-first on the floor and lay there like two bags of rice.

"Note to self," Sammy said as she sat up. "Always tighten laces before entering Fizzy elevator."

"I feel like we've covered this a thousand times," I said.

"Or two thousand," Sammy said. "We've definitely covered it."

"Always tie shoes super tight," I said as we put our shoes back on and yanked them off the gum stuck to the floor. "Come on, let's go find my dad."

We started off through the vast expanse of Fizzopolis. There are giant looping trees everywhere. They're purple and blue and green, and they rise hundreds of feet toward the high ceiling. There are caves and rock formations and a twisty-turny lagoon. There are conveyor belts by the hundreds, moving bottles of Fuzzwonker Fizz from place to place, and the gigantic Fizzomatic machine sits right in the middle of everything.

It's loaded with pipes and buttons and levers. This is the machine that makes Fuzzwonker Fizz, the most popular soda pop in the world. Packed with twenty essential vita-mins and minerals and 100 percent totally sugar-free, its signature feature is the burps it creates. They're the longest ones in the history of burping, and if you get a rare one, they are also unbelievably loud. If you can imagine King Kong belch-ing, it's probably louder than that.

And like I said earlier, the other thing the Fizzomatic machine makes is Fizzies.

"Hi, Franny," I said as we walked past the lagoon. "How's the cleanup going today?"

Franny is one of the many Fizzies in Fizzopolis. She has a hose for a nose so she can suck up water from the lagoon. Franny made a whole bunch of watery snarfing noises.

BuuUUURRRRRRP!

"Sounds like it's going great," Sammy said. I thought so too, since Franny was making happy sounds. She went back to work and we kept walking.

We walked past more caves and trees and a Ping-Pong table. We said hi to a big yellow glob named George, and passed by Kevin, Stacy, and Phil—three more Fizzies who were too busy working to talk. All the Fizzies are different colors and if you pet them they crackle like their fur is carbonated.

There were Fizzies all over the place doing important Fizzopolis work, like making sure

the bottles got labeled correctly. They made sure if you purchased a bottle of Lucy Lemon flavor you didn't end up with Larry Lime instead. Without the Fizzies to help get all the work done, there's no way my dad could keep up with the skyrocketing demand for Fuzzwonker Fizz.

"I'm surprised Floyd hasn't bugged me to use the bathroom," I said as we stared up at my dad's tree house laboratory.

Sammy leaned close to my backpack and listened. "He's making a lot of weird noises in there. Should we check on him?"

"You're right," I agreed, peeling off my backpack and setting it on the ground. "Better if Floyd freaks out down here than up there."

I undid all the knots I'd tied in the strings holding the flap shut. There were at least ten, so it took a while.

"Better stand back," I said. "He's been in there a long time. He might go a little wacky."

Sammy took two steps back as Floyd's green head popped out. He had a rascally look on his face, never a good sign.

"Hey, little buddy," I said. "What was all that about back at school? You almost got me in big trouble."

Floyd's eyes darted back and forth like he was thinking about making a run for it.

"What are you hiding in there?" I asked.

Floyd spoke just loud enough for me to hear him. "Who, me?"

I tried to peek around him into my backpack, but he kept moving to block my view. "Come on, Floyd. What have you got in there?"

Floyd launched into the air three feet over our heads. He did two and a half somersaults and one twist in the pike position like he was in a competitive springboard diving competition, and my bag was a swimming pool.

He landed inside with a thud.

"He's weird," Sammy said.

Both Sammy and I leaned over and looked into the backpack. It was a tight fit for two of us, and we bonked heads. If Floyd tried to jump out of the bag again, he'd have to go through our faces. Double ouch.

"He's trying to hide stuff," Sammy said.

She was right. Floyd was pushing all sorts of things behind my binder and my calculator. It was dark inside the backpack, but it was obvious Floyd was up to no good.

"Come clean, Floyd," I said in my most serious voice.

Floyd got all bashful and stared at his belly button. He stepped away from the corner of my binder and pushed it aside.

"Uh-oh," Sammy said.

"No kidding," I agreed.

There was something in my bag that absolutely-positively-for-sure-without-a-doubt should not have been in there.

About the Author and Artist

PATRICK CARMAN is the *New York Times* best-selling author of the acclaimed series Land of Elyon and Atherton and the teen superhero novel *Thirteen Days to Midnight*. A multimedia pioneer, Patrick authored *The Black Circle*, the fifth title in the 39 Clues series, and the groundbreaking Dark Eden, Skeleton Creek, and Trackers series. An enthusiastic reading advocate, Patrick has visited more than a thousand schools, developed village library projects in Central America, and created author outreach programs for communities. He lives in Walla Walla, Washington, with his family. You can visit him online at www.patrickcarman.com.

BRIAN SHEESLEY is a five-time Emmy Award–winning director, animator, and designer of some of the most popular animated cartoon shows ever, including *Futurama*; *Camp Lazlo!*; *King of the Hill*; *Fanboy and Chum Chum*; *Regular Show*; and *The Simpsons*. He lives in Los Angeles, California, with his family.